# A Rabbit in the sky, OH MI, OH MY!

Sonia B

AuthorHouse™ UK
1663 Liberty Drive
Bloomington, IN 47403 USA
www.authorhouse.co.uk
UK TFN: 0800 0148641 (Toll Free inside the UK)
UK Local: 02036 956322 (+44 20 3695 6322 from outside the UK)

This book is printed on acid-free paper.

ISBN: 978-1-7283-7620-2 (sc)
ISBN: 978-1-7283-7619-6 (e)

Print information available on the last page.

Published by AuthorHouse 10/21/2022

authorHOUSE®

# Acknowledgements

I would like to say thank you to my granddaughter Shaniqua for all the beautiful art work feature in this book.

I would also like to thank Miya and the rest of family for their help and encouragement.

My thanks to all at AuthorHouse Publishing for the support they have given me.

Most of all I must give God thanks for making it all possible.

A rabbit in the sky—oh me, oh my!

A rabbit in the sky—oh me, oh my!

Way up high on the cloud.

Rabbit always gets himself into mischief.

He finds everything fun.

He sees a balloon stuck in the shrub and tugs on it.

And—whoops—now he is on a cloud in the sky way up high.

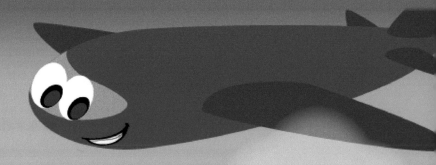

Mrs Plane passes by, giving him a fright.

"Mrs Plane, stop! Please stop—I need a ride."

So also shouts Master Guinea Pig, "Plane, plane!"

Master Guinea Pig is a copycat.

Everything Rabbit does, he does too,

So it is no surprise that they are both in the same pickle.

They shout at the plane,

"Mrs Plane, Mrs Plane!

"We are too high for a bus or a train."

The plane zooms by—

"Oh mi, oh my," they sigh.

Then Miss Cow comes along.

"H-hey, Mr Rabbit! H-hey, Mr Guinea Pig!"

"Hi, Miss Cow."

"Why are you t-two so sad?"

"The plane did not stop."

"That's n-no shock."

"What do you mean?" say the chaps.

"I ran so fast upon a cloud,

"B-built up some steam—M-mum would be proud.

"But to my surprise, the sun was out."

"That is good," the other two exclaim.

"N-no, n-no!" shouts Miss Cow. "I was hoping to jump the moon,

"Not sunbathe at noon."

Miss Cow reckons he has superpowers because he can jump as high as a plane.

But all the other animals call him No Brain.

As far back as he can remember, Miss Cow has talked with a stammer.

This does not stop him from getting up to tricks.

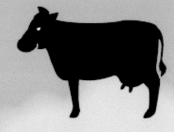

"Hello, you lot!"

They all look 'round.

"Hi, Mr Crane!" They all greet him in unison,

Grinning.

Mr Crane looks puzzled. "Thanks for the welcome, guys!

"To what do I owe such an honour?"

Mr Crane is no bird brain, and his thinking is as sharp as a razor.

He thinks on his feet.

"Our saving grace, our safe way down to the ground!"

They say, still speaking all together.

They broaden their grins.

"Oh no, oh no," Mr Crane begins to explain. "I am not a plane!

"Any fool can see there is no engine in my body."

Mr Crane's business head starts working straightaway.

It starts to take over.

"Okay, guys, what's in it for me?"

"Birdseed galore and fish for sure."

"Come on, you guys; you cannot fool me.

"Where will you get such bounty to feed me?"

"Farmer Bill will be so glad to see us that he will thank you

"With bucket loads of stuff."

Mr Crane is feeling good now;

He loves fish and birdseed. His belly is rumbling, and it tickles him.

Mr Crane can't resist food.

"Hop on, guys!

"Hold on tight—

"Here we go!"

"Whee!"

When they land on the farm and all settle down for the night,

Mr Rabbit says, "Night-night, you guys."

He settles down and dreams of his next adventure and wonders where it will take him. Soon, with a smile, he is fast asleep.

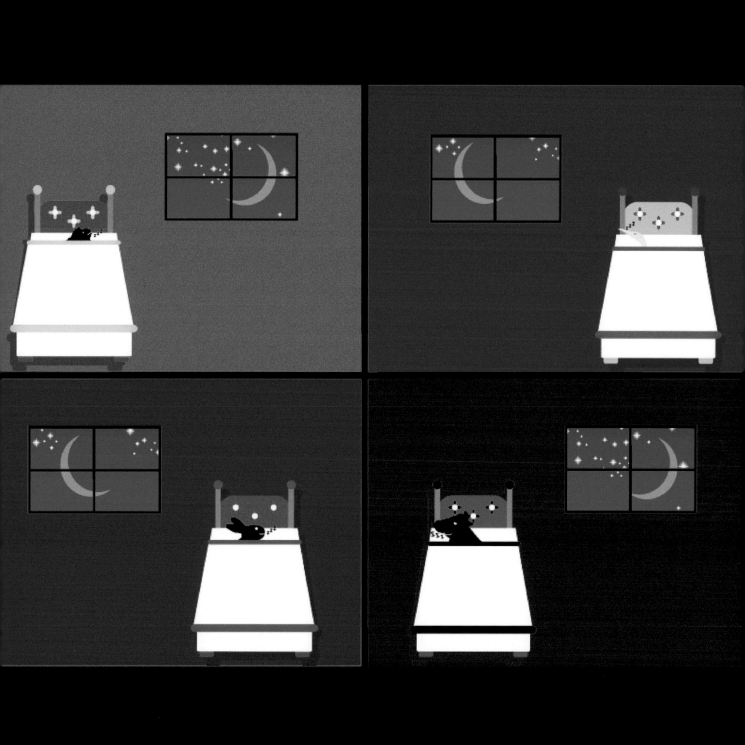